DATE DUE

MAI APR 30 1990	MAI JUL 29 1991
MAI JUN 0 2 1990	NOV 0 7 1994
MAIOCT 2 1 1990	JUL 1 2 1995
	MAI SEP 0 5 1995
FEB 0 8 1991	OCT 2 1 1995
MAI APR 0 6 1991	AUG 0 4 1995
MAI APR 1 6 1991	
MAI AUG 30 1991	
MAI FEB 0 2 1993	
MAI MAR 0 9 1993	
MAI MAY 1 6 1993	
FEB 0 4 1995	
MAI JUL 2 9 1995	

5.6

Saint George
and the Dragon

Written by Geraldine McCaughrean
Illustrated by Nicki Palin

DOUBLEDAY
NEW YORK LONDON TORONTO SYDNEY AUCKLAND

THE still, deep pool lay in a hollow below the high wooden fence of the hilltop town. Every day the women came down to draw its water. Their sheep drank at its banks, and a few straggling roses bloomed, in coils of bramble, along the water's edge.

Then, one morning, the women walking down to the water dropped their empty buckets, ran back, and closed the city gates, sobbing with fright. Climbing to the top of the palisade, they peeped over.

A dragon, born in the deepest crevices of the bottomless pool, had dragged itself out onto the bank and lay coiled around it.

A wreath of sinew and claw. Its red mouth gaped as it panted in the hot sun. Its ragged teeth bulged through rolled green lips. And awake or asleep, its lidless eyes stared and its claws stretched and withdrew, stretched and withdrew in the waterside mud. Its foul breath hung in a green haze. Its father was Evil, its mother Darkness, and its name was Wickedness.

That night it left the pool, lifting its heavy haunches and heaving its scaled belly off the ground. Lizard-like, it cut a track through the mud, dragging its thorny tail. The people herded their livestock into the city and shut the gates on the dragon.

But what good is a wooden fence
against breath fuming with fire?
One corner of the town was set ablaze,
and its crumbling ash blew away in the
morning wind.

The dragon ate two dogs, before
thrashing back to the pool to coil itself
around the water.

The next day, the people opened the gates
just wide enough to push two sheep out onto
the plain. The animals stood bleating,
then trotted down toward the water in the
hollow. Suddenly, the shape of the dragon
lurched up over them! Fleece and flesh,
it tore them to pieces.

Two sheep were fed to the dragon
every day, though sometimes, after its meal,
it would still slither toward the city and
scratch its back against the timber fence.

From the high window of the palace, Princess Sabra watched with a pale face, and asked, "What will happen when there are no more sheep?"

Before the last sheep was gone, the people began to draw lots in the most terrible of lotteries. The name of every man, woman, and child was entered, and one name drawn out each day: one person to be turned out of the city, side by side with a sheep as food for the dragon.

Soon, the sound of wailing hung like a cloud over the city. Men eyed one another across the street and thought, "I hope his name will be drawn before mine."

One day, the wailing came from the palace itself. The Princess Sabra's name had been drawn in the lottery.

"No! I forbid it!" cried the King.

"It is the law," said the town governors. "You made it so."

"But she is so good and pure, and I love her so very much!"

"We loved our daughters," said the old women, "but still they were fed to the dragon when their turn came."

"But she's so small and fragile—a poor morsel for a hungry dragon!"

"Then go in her place!" shouted the people. "What good have you been to us since the dragon came?"

And when he saw rebellion in their faces, the King gave up his daughter. "Don't let me see her again, or I may change my mind."

Not far away, a horseman was riding
up a steep hill when his horse stopped and
began to paw the ground, blowing sharply through
its nostrils. The rider himself was aware of a charred,
acrid smell in the air. From the top of the hill,
he looked down on devastation.

In the hollow below, there lay a fouled and festering pool. Beyond it, a fortified town had its gates closed in siege.

Turning its head idly in his direction, a dragon, its flightless wings half spread, paused in its slinking, lizard-like scuttle, and let out a roar.

The flash of sunlight on a bridle, and the white of the horse itself, had caught the dragon's eye. At the same moment, a speck of white and gold flickered to its left: a golden-haired maiden dressed in a lightly blowing smock was being tied to the stake where the beast looked daily for its dinner.

The girl cast one imploring look toward the town. But the windows of her father's palace were empty. Her head fell forward in despair.

The dragon threw out a contemptuous roar at the rider and turned to devour its white morsel of meat. . . .

"Hear this, beast, that I am George of Lydda, and a pure man!"
The rider's voice barely reached the dragon across the wilderness.
"Turn and fight me—for surely your father was Evil, your mother
Darkness, and you are Wickedness itself!" George leveled his long
lance.

The dragon's jaw—gaping over the Princess—clashed shut.
It snaked on its haunches, and its wings beat the air.

A column of fuming fire belched from its nostrils.
But the soldier, galloping toward it across the plain,
raised a shield over his own and his horse's head,
and the fire was turned aside. The brightness
of the sun on shield and helmet seemed to
madden the rampaging beast.

George's noble white horse carried him into the very
shadow of the dragon. Its green paw reached out to snatch
him from his saddle. The lance slapped the dragon's
shoulder, but the scales were tough like leather,
rough like stone.

Horse and dragon cannoned together. The mare's
foamy sweat spattered the dragon's green flank.
A moment later, the massive tail lashed round,
but the horse stood back on its haunches
and sprang across its thorns.

George's lance struck the beast's snout
and shattered like an icicle.

For a moment, he stared into the lidless eyes, then he threw up his shield again, to keep off the caldron breath.

The dragon struck him a blow with its horny wing that pitched him to the ground. George threw off his helmet, and snatched the broad sword from his saddle.

As vast jaws opened to devour the soldier where he stood, he ran in under the towering green chest and plunged in the sword where a heart should lie.

But the creature had no heart!

A spurt of black blood spattered George's shield. But the
dragon only threw back its head and gave a gargled roar.
Its claws tore the young man's cloak into seven ragged strips.

Once more George drove in the sword—drove it
into the gaping red jaw. It was torn from his grasp
as the beast thrashed its head from side to side.

For a moment, the lumbering body
threatened to capsize and crush George.
And as he put both hands on the
dragon's flank to push it away,
smoke rose from the palms
of his gloves. With the
groaning slowness of a
falling tree, the creature
crashed down onto
its side.

George left it where it lay, and ran to the side
of the Princess, lifted up her face, and said,
"The danger is almost past. I see that you are
a pure and lovely maiden. Give me your sash,
please, for the dragon is not dead."
With the sash, he circled the lolling
green head.

In the depths of the beast's cavernous body, its furious fire was extinguished. In the depths of its eyes, too, the wildness and wickedness went out. The vanquished dragon laid down its head on George's lap, its breathing calm, its breath harmless to the sweet and unscorched air.

Together, Sabra and George led a peaceful dragon through the streets of the town and it lay down at the gates of the palace.

"Stranger," said the delighted King, "where you are from I do not know. But end your journey here, with my palace for your home and my daughter for your wife!"

"I cannot," said George, though he looked at the Princess with longing in his eyes. "I have other dragons to vanquish."

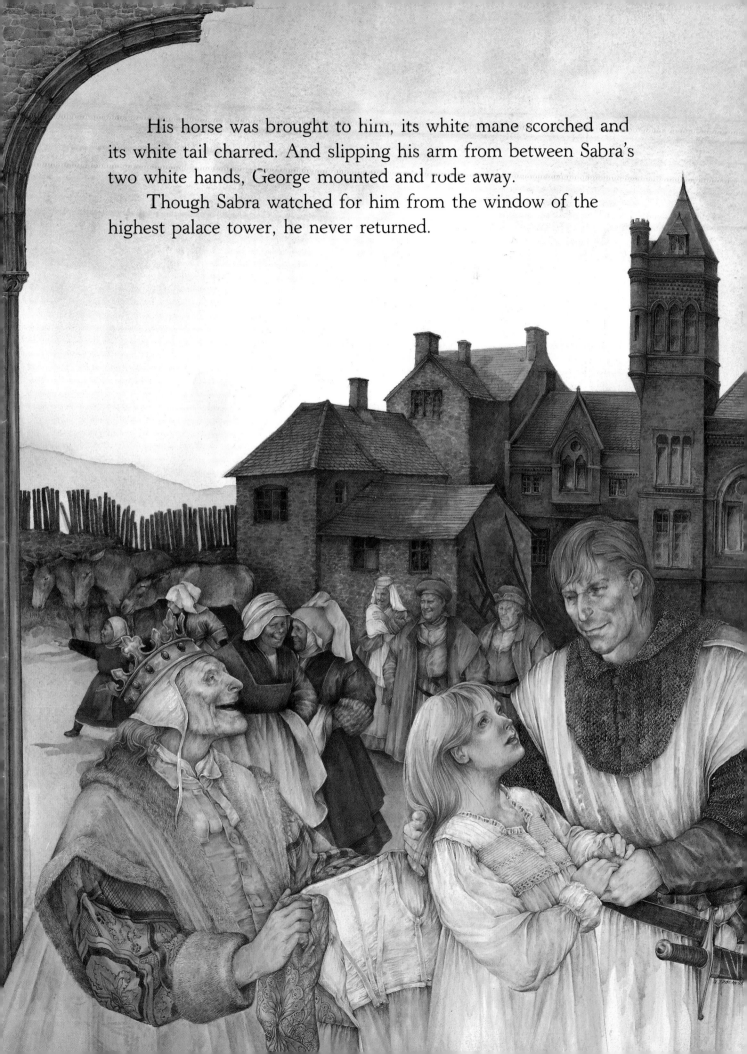

His horse was brought to him, its white mane scorched and
its white tail charred. And slipping his arm from between Sabra's
two white hands, George mounted and rode away.

Though Sabra watched for him from the window of the
highest palace tower, he never returned.

Some people say that he took ship and traveled to other countries and fought other dragons.

Even after a thousand years, some said they had seen him, still wielding his sword and blood-splashed shield, still fighting dragony Death.

But no memory survives of the place where George finally laid down his sword and slept.

Some say his grave lies in Persia in a place where bloodred roses flourish their blossoms through toils of briar, beside still, deep water.

English soldiers, returning from a brutal
and bloody war, swore they had seen George—
his white banner crossed with blood—and
that his encouragement had saved them.
In gratitude, they blazoned the memory
of him on their armor and their flags,
and called him England's own
Saint George.

AFTERWORD

The details of the life of George the Saint are few and uncertain. It is thought that he was executed by the Roman Emperor Diocletian on April 23, A.D. 303, but no one knows for certain. Many Christians were executed in those days and few records remain. But that George lived and died is proven. His death is commemorated on St. George's Day.

Stories relating George the Dragon Slayer's remarkable adventures were widely told in the Middle East over a thousand years ago. The English Crusaders brought these fantastic tales home with them and even added a story of their own, telling how St. George had appeared to them in a vision at the battle of Antioch in 1098.

Medieval English people acted out George's adventures in miracle plays and pictured him in their church windows. He so captured their hearts that in 1348 Edward III made him the patron saint of England.

Published by Doubleday, a division of Bantam Doubleday Dell Publishing Group, Inc. 666 Fifth Avenue, New York, New York 10103 **Doubleday** and the portrayal of an anchor with a dolphin are trademarks of Doubleday, a division of Bantam Doubleday Dell Publishing Group, Inc. Library of Congress Cataloging-in-Publication Data. McCaughrean, Geraldine. Saint George and the dragon. Summary: A rendition of the legend of Saint George, recounting how the brave, mysterious horseman saved a city from a terrible dragon. 1. George, Saint, d. 303—Legends. [1. George, Saint, d. 303. 2. Folklore—England. 3. Knights and knighthood—Folklore. 4. Dragons—Folklore] I. Palin, Nicki, ill. II. Title. PZ8.1.M144Sai 1989 398.2′1′0942 89-1538 ISBN 0-385-26528-X ISBN 0-385-26529-8 (lib. bdg.) Illustrations copyright © 1989 by Nicki Palin. Text copyright © 1989 by Geraldine McCaughrean All Rights Reserved. Printed in Hong Kong. First Edition in the United States of America, 1989 0989